Click, Clack, Surprise!

Click, Clack,
SURPRISE!

Doreen Cronin
Illustrated by **Betsy Lewin**

Ready-to-Read

Simon Spotlight

New York   London   Toronto   Sydney   New Delhi

For Ryleigh Elizabeth —D. C.

For Ted, who has had eighty surprises so far —B. L.

SIMON SPOTLIGHT
An imprint of Simon & Schuster Children's Publishing Division
1230 Avenue of the Americas, New York, New York 10020
This Simon Spotlight edition May 2019 • Text copyright © 2016 by Doreen Cronin • Illustrations copyright © 2016 by Betsy Lewin
All rights reserved, including the right of reproduction in whole or in part in any form. SIMON SPOTLIGHT, READY-TO-READ,
and colophon are registered trademarks of Simon & Schuster, Inc. For information about special discounts for bulk purchases,
please contact Simon & Schuster Special Sales at 1-866-506-1949 or business@simonandschuster.com.
This Simon & Schuster Speakers Bureau can bring authors to your live event. For more information or to book an event contact
the Simon & Schuster Speakers Bureau at 1-866-248-3049 or visit our website at www.simonspeakers.com.
Manufactured in the United States of America 0419 LAK
10 9 8 7 6 5 4 3 2 1
Cataloging-In-Publication Data is available from the Library of Congress.
ISBN 978-1-5344-1383-2 (hc)
ISBN 978-1-5344-1382-5 (pbk)
ISBN 978-1-5344-1384-9 (eBook)

Click, Clack, Surprise!

It is a very big day on the farm.
A cake is baking.
Streamers are streaming.
Mice are floating past the window.

The invitations have
been delivered.

~~Pin the Tail on the Donkey~~
Canceled by Donkey.

~~Duck,~~
~~Duck~~
~~Goose~~
Canceled
by Goose.

~~Steal the Bacon~~
Canceled by
Secret
Someone.

Everybody wants to look their best for Little Duck's party.

Duck takes a long, hot bubble bath to look his best.

He rub-a-dubs,

rub-a-dubs,

rub-a-dubs clean.

And walks on over to the maple tree.

Little Duck watches
and then rub-a-dubs too.

The sheep need a trim
to look their best.

They snippity-clip,
snippity-clip,
snippity-clip clean.

And walk on over to the maple tree.

Little Duck watches
and then snippity-clips too.

The cat wants to look her best.

She slurp-a-lurps,

slurp-a-lurps,

slurp-a-lurps clean.

And walks on over to the maple tree.

Little Duck watches
and then slurp-a-lurps too.

The chickens take a dust bath
to look their best.

They shimmy-shake,

shimmy-shake,
 shimmy-shake clean.

And walk on over to the maple tree.

Little Duck watches
and then shimmy-shakes too.

The pigs need a mud bath
to feel their best.

They squish and squash,

squish and squash,
squish and squash clean.

And walk on over to the maple tree.

Little Duck watches
and then squishes
and squashes too.

The cows like themselves
just the way they are.

No rub-a-dubbing.
  No snippity-clipping.
    No slurp-a-lurping.
      No shimmy-shaking.
        No squish and squashing.

They walk on over to the maple tree.

Farmer Brown frosts the cake,

lights the candles,

puts on his best hat,

and walks on over to the maple tree.

Happy
Birthday
to you,

Happy Birthday to...

ewww!

A birthday surprise for *everyone*, under the maple tree.